Mittens

Your Cat's Wild Cousins

Also by Hope Ryden

Wild Animals of America ABC
Wild Animals of Africa ABC

The Little Deer of the Florida Keys
Bobcat
America's Bald Eagle
The Beaver

Your Cat's Wild Cousins

photographs and text by
Hope Ryden

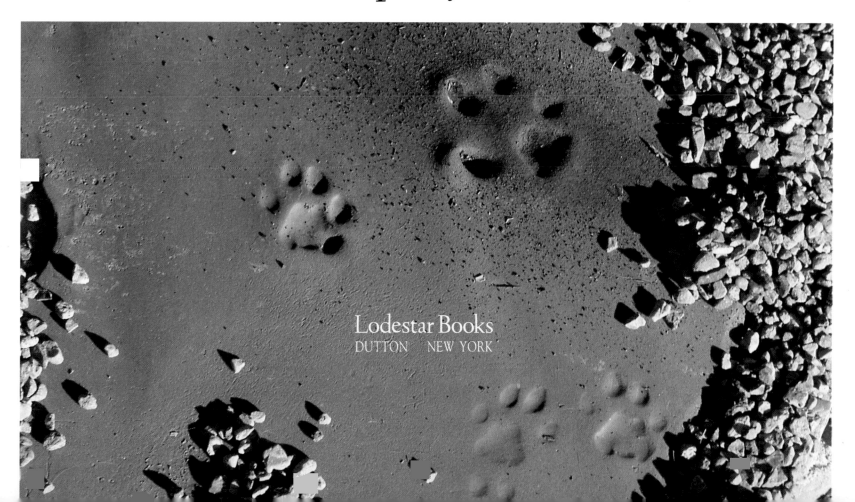

Lodestar Books
DUTTON   NEW YORK

for Lily, who found me, and all the stray cats like her
who are looking for a home

Library of Congress Cataloging-in-Publication Data
Ryden, Hope.
Your cat's wild cousins / text and photographs by Hope Ryden.—1st ed.
p. cm.
Includes index.
Summary: Similarities and differences between domestic cats and various types of wild cats
that inhabit the Earth are explored.
ISBN 0-525-67354-7
1. Felidae—Juvenile literature. 2. Cats—Juvenile literature.
[1. Cats. 2. Felidae.]
QL737.C23R93 1991
599.74'428—dc20

90-28992
CIP
AC

Published in the United States by Lodestar Books,
an affiliate of Dutton Children's Books, a division of Penguin Books USA Inc.
375 Hudson Street, New York, New York 10014

Published simultaneously in Canada by McClelland & Stewart, Toronto

Editor: Virginia Buckley Designer: Richard Granald, LMD

Printed in Hong Kong First Edition 10 9 8 7 6 5 4 3 2 1

Acknowledgments

A number of the cats in this book were photographed in the wild. Some species, however, have become so endangered that it is impractical to search for them in their shrinking habitats. Many are rare even in captivity. The world's zoo population of black-footed cats, for example, numbers only thirty-one; and there are only twelve Pallas's cats in captivity. I found both of these species at the Cincinnati Zoo, which has the finest collection of small cats in the world. My thanks to the Cincinnati Zoo for its commitment to preserve these beautiful creatures. I am also grateful to Dan Wharton of The Bronx Zoo for directing me to this source and for locating another hard-to-find cat. The San Diego Zoo, it turns out, is the only place in the country where the domestic cat's immediate ancestor, the African wildcat, can be found. Staff at the San Diego Zoo were very helpful in providing background information and allowing me to photograph this animal close up. Finally, I wish to thank personnel at the Alberta Wildlife Park, near Edmonton, Canada, for their hospitality during the unbearably hot day I spent photographing a jaguar.

Contents

Domestic Cat

This is Lily. She is a domestic cat, that is, she makes her home with people (namely me). Unlike her wild relatives, she doesn't have to catch her own food. I provide her meals and give her shelter. Even so, she has much in common with cats in the wild who do make their own living. Like the lion, she is very good at sneaking up on prey. Like the puma, she keeps her claws sharpened and ready for action. And like the fishing cat, she takes good care of her fur, even when I forget to brush her.

The scientific name for the domestic cat is *Felis catus*. People have bred *Felis catus* to look many ways. Some have long hair, some have short hair, some have no hair at all. Others are spotted, or striped, or all one color. Whatever type of coat your cat has does not change the fact that he or she is a domestic cat. So, even though your pet cat may not look exactly like mine, he or she is certain to act like her. For example, your cat probably likes to chase moving objects. So does Lily. That's because long ago, before cats came to live with human beings, their ancestors had to hunt small animals for food. Today Lily is served her dinner in a bowl, but she still has what it takes to catch a meal.

Did you ever wonder how it happened that the domestic cat came to live with people?

African Wildcat

Nearly all scientists agree that the African wildcat is the ancestor of our present-day house cat. It certainly looks like it could be somebody's tabby! But who tamed this beautiful wild animal? And how long ago?

The earliest evidence of a domestic cat was found in a 4000-year-old Egyptian tomb, which contained seventeen of their skeletons. Alongside the remains of each cat was a pot for milk to nourish it in the afterworld. From that time on, pet cats appeared in many Egyptian paintings. One 3600-year-old picture shows a cat tied to its owner's chair with a red ribbon.

No one knows just how the first cat was tamed. Perhaps an Egyptian farmer saw an African wildcat catch a rat or a mouse that was eating up his precious grain and set out bowls of sheep's milk to attract more of these mousers to his barns. Perhaps a mother wildcat brought her kittens to drink the sheep's milk set out by the farmer. Maybe the farmer's son caught the wild kittens and brought them home.

No matter how it happened, once the cat was tamed it was destined for greatness. The Egyptian people came to think of it as a god and passed laws to protect it. Anyone who harmed a cat was put to death. Even poor people were expected to give their pet cats expensive burials. Every casket had to be painted to look like the animal inside. Sometimes precious jewels were used as eyes. One ancient tomb in Benii Hasan, Egypt, contained 80,000 cat mummies. No one counted all the mouse mummy dinners that had been buried with them!

Today the untamed ancestor of the domestic cat still exists in out-of-the-way places in Africa. It is an excellent hunter and feeds on all kinds of rodents and birds. Sometimes it eats snakes and lizards. Its future is uncertain though. Human beings have taken over land that is needed by the African wildcat. To make matters worse, free-roaming house cats often mate with it, and the kittens that result are neither wild nor tame. Many people fear that the African wildcat will soon vanish from the earth. Wouldn't it be a shame if the animal that gave rise to our wonderful pet cat were to become extinct?

Does Lily look like the African wildcat?

🐾 The scientific name for the African wildcat is *Felis silvestris lybica*. It lives in all parts of Africa.

11

Lion

Your cat's most awesome cousin is certainly the lion. This wild cat is known as King of the Beasts—and for good reason. A lion is so powerful that it can knock over and kill a buffalo. Its roar sounds like a cathedral organ and can be heard for five miles. And no cat wears such a handsome mane as does this mighty hunter. The lion's most remarkable trait, however, is neither its strength nor

its good looks. The lion is different from all other members of the cat family in that it likes company. Instead of living alone, adult lions link up with one another to form groups, called prides.

A lion pride is formed by two or more adult females, or lionesses, who stay together for life. Their friendships are so strong that they even nurse one another's cubs. These females are joined by males who remain with them for as long as they are able. Sooner or later, however, younger, stronger males overthrow them and take over the pride. A pride of lions may number as many as thirty. Usually it is made up of four to fifteen animals. When male lions lose their place in a pride, they continue to live and hunt together, like the two pictured on this page.

Males who live in a pride have an easy life, because most of the stalking and killing is done by the females. Lionesses are skilled at this. They work together to encircle a herd of antelopes or zebras. Each lioness knows exactly where to position herself. To avoid being seen, she crawls to her post on her belly. When all are in place, one lioness sneaks—oh so carefully—to the downwind side of the herd. Then in a sudden rush she drives a victim toward her waiting sisters.

After a kill has been made, the males and the cubs join the lionesses for dinner. Because male lions are bigger and stronger than females, they often claim the whole carcass, forcing the lionesses—who did all the work—to wait for leftovers. This behavior has given rise to the popular expression "getting the lion's share."

Does your cat stalk moving objects?

🐾 The scientific name for the lion is *Panthera leo*. It lives mainly in Africa. The Asian lion has become rare.

Caracal

The caracal is the perkiest member of the cat kingdom. It struts and poses and waves its rather short tail like some kind of cartoon character. When something attracts its attention, it cocks its head like a dog. The caracal's tufted ears give it a saucy look, as if the tufts were feathers in its cap.

This cat is full of life and a delight to watch. Sometimes it dashes this way and that for no apparent reason. But the caracal is rarely seen because it lives in rocky deserts where humans do not like to go. During the heat of the day it takes refuge in caves and crevices. At night it hunts. Its large tufted ears help it pick up sounds of animals scurrying among the desert plants.

The caracal is a superb hunter. It preys on hares and small antelopes, and is so agile that it can catch birds by leaping straight up in the air and batting them to the ground with its big front paws. It has even been known to overpower fierce eagles when they roost in trees.

This medium-sized cousin of your cat and mine can be tamed. In times past, people in India and Iran trained the caracal to hunt birds and small game for them.

14

Would your cat catch birds if she had a chance?

🐾 The scientific name for the caracal is *Caracal caracal*. It lives in Africa, the Middle East, and southern Asia.

15

Cheetah

The fastest cat in the world is the cheetah. It can run seventy miles an hour. It can sail twenty-three feet in a single leap. It can zigzag after darting antelopes without losing its footing. From a complete standstill, it is able to reach a speed of forty miles an hour in just two seconds. The most powerful sports car cannot do that!

Even though the cheetah is fast, it tires quickly. That is why it does not waste energy chasing animals that have a long head start on it. Instead, it waits behind cover until a herd of antelopes or gazelles comes close to its hiding place. Then, in a sudden burst of energy, it runs one of them down.

Cheetah mothers bring food for their cubs until they are two years old and able to run down and catch animals by themselves. Then the youngsters must strike out on their own. The females go their separate ways. Male cubs, however, stay together for life. Cheetah brothers fight and hunt as a team.

The cheetah differs from all other members of the cat kingdom in that its claws resemble those of a dog: They cannot be withdrawn into protective covers. Your cat and mine keep their claws in sheaths and bring them out only when needed. That way they remain sharp. Though the cheetah's constantly extended claws help it grip the ground when running, such hard use dulls them. As a result, they make poor killing tools. Nor are they much help to the cheetah when lions or a pack of hyenas try to rob it of its catch. That explains why this large cat often gives up a hard-won dinner without putting up a fight.

Today the cheetah is rare. Much of the land it needs to live on has been turned into farms. And untold numbers of these cats have been shot for their beautiful skins. Some people think that by wearing the cheetah's fur coat, they will look as elegant as it does. What do you think?

Are your cat's claws sharp? How does she keep them that way?

The scientific name for the cheetah is *Acinonyx jubatus*. It lives only on Africa's shrinking savannah lands. Because these grassy plains are good for farming, human beings are taking them over. The cheetah is on the endangered species list and may soon become extinct.

Black-Footed Cat

The black-footed cat is the smallest cat in the world. It is smaller, by far, than your pet cat or mine. Most domestic cats weigh between seven and twelve pounds. The black-footed cat tips the scale at four! Such a tiny creature has to have a lot of nerve to make its living by hunting. But, of course, it has no choice. It is a carnivore, or meat-eater. If it did not kill and eat other animals, it would starve.

Like all young cats, black-footed babies are playful. But their games are more advanced than those of domestic kittens. While still very young, they begin to stalk and eat a great many insects. As a result, they are able to kill small animals when only forty-three days old.

Even so, they stay with their mother for many months. If she senses danger, she makes a special cry, which tells them to "scatter and hide." Afterward she calls them back with another "all clear" sound. In this respect, she behaves more like a grouse or a pheasant than a cat. All other cat mothers, when alarmed, send their litters to their nest. Maybe the black-footed cat is the wisest mother of all. If one of her kittens is discovered, the others may still escape being noticed.

It should come as no surprise that the soles of the black-footed cat's feet are black. But did you know that what we take to be a cat's lower leg is really its foot? Cats walk on their tiptoes. Can you see the long black foot of the cat that is scratching itself in this picture?

Does your cat catch and eat bugs like her cousin the black-footed cat?

The scientific name for the black-footed cat is *Felis nigripes*. It lives in the southern part of Africa.

19

Serval

The serval is shaped like no other cat. Its legs appear too long for its body. Its ears look much too big for its head. Still the serval is a lovely-looking animal. More important, its long legs enable it to soar over the tops of the tall grasses that grow on the African savannah, where it lives. With each bound, it is carried many feet forward. In addition, its big ears pick up the faint noises made by small animals threading through the dense savannah grasses. Guided only by sound, this long-legged, big-eared hunter strikes. High in the

air it leaps, then comes down on its two front paws, pinning its victim to the ground. In so doing, the serval looks like a diver, who gains lift from a springboard before plunging headfirst into the water.

Like most cats, the adult serval lives and hunts by itself. Only during mating season does it seek out its own kind. At such times two males may get into a fight over a female, like the cats pictured here. Whichever one wins the battle will father the kittens. He will not, however, remain with the mother serval to help her raise their young. That she does all by herself.

Because it is so long-legged, the serval lies down like a dog with its front legs outstretched. Most medium- and small-sized cats prefer to tuck their forepaws under their chests, or sometimes they rest in a crouched position.

How does your cat lie down?

🐾 The scientific name for the serval is *Leptailurus serval*. It lives in Africa.

21

Leopard

If ever a cat could be described as "the most," it is the leopard. It is the most stealthy, the most secretive, and the most adaptable, and it comes in the most sizes and patterns of any of the world's cats. Some people even think it is the most beautiful.

Just how stealthy is the leopard?

The leopard is able to creep near enough to a flighty gazelle or an alert antelope to catch it in a single pounce.

But is it really more secretive than any other wild cat?

Maybe not, but judge for yourself. Leopards have been discovered living in major African cities without anybody suspecting it!

Certainly no one can deny that the leopard is adaptable. Whereas the cheetah must live on savannah land and the caracal likes a dry, rocky habitat, the leopard does well anywhere. It can live in swamplands, on mountaintops, in jungles, on grassy savannahs, and in hardwood forests. Its range stretches across most of Africa, and includes much of the Middle East and Asia, as well.

Finally, when it comes to the matter of dress, the leopard must be the most original. No two leopards wear the same spots. Some sport mostly round polka dots. Others have a greater number of floral patterns. Still others come in solid black. Black leopards, also known as panthers, were once thought to be a separate species. Now we know that cubs from the same litter can be black or spotted. What's more, a black panther's coat never completely hides the animal's true identity. In the right light, a faint tracing of spots always shows through.

As if these traits aren't enough to set the leopard apart from other cats, here's another: In the big-cat class (which includes lions, tigers, cheetahs, jaguars, and leopards) only the leopard makes regular use of trees. It can leap to a high branch with the greatest of ease. It can even haul a large animal it has killed up with it. High in a treetop, where it is safe from lions or hyenas or wild dogs who might try to steal its catch, the leopard looks down on the rest of the animal kingdom. Maybe the leopard knows that it is "the most."

Does your cat like to get up into trees like a leopard?

🐾 The scientific name for the leopard is *Panthera pardus*. Its range includes most of Africa, the Middle East, and southern Asia.

Tiger

The scientific name for the tiger is *Panthera tigris*. It lives only in Asia. Once it could be found in the north, south, east, and west of that big continent. Now it survives mainly in India and Nepal, where reserves have been established to protect it. It is seriously endangered.

The tiger is the largest member of the cat family. Some male tigers in Siberia are thirteen feet long and weigh as much as six hundred pounds. Such a big predator has to kill large animals or it will go hungry. Since the tiger is the most powerful of cats, it is able to do that. It can kill an elephant, a buffalo, a bear, even a rhinoceros—and without the help of another tiger!

Because tigers live and hunt alone, they have developed many clever strategies for bringing down prey. For example, a tiger will sometimes hide beside a pond or a river. When animals come to drink, it singles one out and chases it into deep water. There the tiger, who is an excellent swimmer, holds its victim underwater until it stops struggling.

As a result of human activities, much of the tiger's natural prey has vanished. In India, where tigers were once common, forests have been cut, and forest animals have been replaced by domestic livestock. Only a few thousand tigers remain, and some of these now kill and eat bullocks and cows to survive. Such behavior does not make them popular with farmers, especially since a hungry tiger may, on occasion, attack a human being. Many Indian farm workers wear a face mask on the back of their head to fool any lurking tiger into thinking it is being watched. Like all cats, tigers prefer to sneak up on their prey.

When one tiger tries to steal another tiger's meal, a fight is almost certain to erupt. But the tiger has a tender side, too. No animal is more attentive to her babies than a mother tigress. She hunts for them until they are almost two years old. And she does not take a bite of

24

what she has killed until they have eaten their fill. What's more, if anyone or anything threatens her cubs, she turns into a striped fury. That is why women who are quick to defend their children are said to act like "mother tigers."

Though all tigers are striped, no two look alike. Each one's stripes are of different lengths and widths. For that matter, not all tigers are black and orange. In recent years some have been discovered with brown stripes on a white background—like the family pictured here.

Is your cat striped like a tiger?

25

Marbled Cat

The marbled cat is not well known, perhaps because it is so hard to see. It lives in the treetops of Southeast Asia and spends most of each day and night resting on lofty branches. It is designed to escape notice. Its dappled coat blends with the mix of sunlight and shadow that filters through the leaves. About the only way you can spot this cat is to look for a long, fat tail dangling from a branch.

The marbled cat's tail is unique in the cat kingdom. It is so long and so thick, you'd think a very large cat was attached to it. Not so. The marbled cat is only slightly bigger than your cat and mine. Its oversized tail serves as a balancing rod when this tree-dweller chases birds and squirrels from branch to branch.

Most animals that hunt in the dark have eyes that glow like hot coals when a light is shined on them. That is because their eyes contain cells that act like tiny mirrors to magnify whatever light there is. Such eyes help the marbled cat catch food in the shadowy jungle. Even on the darkest night it has no difficulty spotting prey, for it sees a much brighter world than you or I do.

Little is known about this secretive cat. One lucky observer reports that it has a fierce nature. Whether or not this is true, one thing is certain: The marbled cat does not look for trouble. Otherwise more people would have had the good fortune of seeing it.

Do your cat's eyes glow when a light is shined on them?

 The scientific name for the marbled cat is *Pardofelis marmorata*. It is found in Southeast Asia and parts of Nepal and Sikkim.

27

Pallas's Cat

At first glance, Pallas's cat looks more like a monkey than a cat. Its face is flat, and its ears are set on the sides of its head instead of on top. Of course, there is a practical reason for this. Pallas's cat lives on rocky slopes, where there are few plants or bushes to hide behind. As a result, it has to sight prey across the tops of rocks. If its ears were like those of other cats, every mouse, hare, or rock rabbit would notice them sticking up and dive into a hole.

Pallas's cat has been shaped by its rugged home in other ways as well. It lives in remote parts of Russia where winters are harsh and cold. To keep warm, it grows long, dense fur, especially on its underbelly. This keeps it warm when crouching in snow, waiting to dash at prey. Its short, stout legs help it maintain a firm footing on rugged slopes. Even its temperament has been affected by its barren surroundings. Without handy trees to climb or underbrush to hide in, this small cat has to stand its ground when other animals threaten it. No wonder it is quick to show its temper.

28

While I was photographing this cousin of your cat and mine, it made several rushes at me, all the while grimacing and producing an explosive-sounding huff. Chances are it was putting on an act, though, for records show that Pallas's cat can be tamed and kept as a pet.

When your cat hides in underbrush, do you see her ears?

The scientific name for Pallas's cat is *Felis (Otocolobus) manul*. It lives in Asia.

29

Snow Leopard

The snow leopard makes its home in the tallest mountain range in the world, the Himalayas. No other cat lives at such high elevations. A mountain climber who wishes to scale these towering peaks needs to train for weeks beforehand. Even then, he or she must carry oxygen to help breathe the thin air.

In summer the snow leopard visits the highest part of these mountains. There, trees do not grow and much of the ground remains covered with snow all year round. To obtain dinner, this big cat hunts snowcocks and marmots. Or it stalks wild tahr and ibex that leap about on the steep rock slides. Only an expert jumper like the snow leopard would dare pursue these sure-footed creatures in such dangerous places.

The snow leopard is the champion jumper of all the world's cats. In one bound it can cover a distance of forty-nine feet! Its long tail helps it recover its balance when making a difficult landing. Snow leopard cubs, like the ones in this picture, must learn to move about on slippery rocks while still very young.

Though the snow leopard is a powerful athlete, it poses no threat to human beings. There is no record of anyone ever being attacked by this lover of high places.

How does your cat feel about snow?

 The scientific name for the snow leopard is *Uncia uncia*. It lives in the highest mountains in the world, the Himalayas of Asia.

Fishing Cat

Most house cats do not like baths. They don't need them. They do a wonderful job of keeping themselves clean with their tongues. A cat's tongue is covered with rasps that scrape away every bit of dirt that clings to its coat. Try to give your pet cat a bath and you may have a struggle on your hands. Even

though some cats like to play with a dripping faucet, only a rare kitty will allow itself to be plunged into a basin of water.

Your cat has one wild cousin, however, that doesn't mind getting wet at all. The fishing cat of Southeast Asia lives in marshes and along coastal creeks. There it hunts frogs and mollusks in shallow water, and dives into deep pools to catch fish. The fishing cat is well equipped for this kind of life. It has developed webs between its toes to help it paddle fast. Its eyes flick about in their sockets more than do those of other cats. This helps it to keep darting fish in sight. What's more, it has no fear of dunking its whole head underwater.

Like a human fisherman, the fishing cat knows more than one way to make a catch. Sometimes it sits perfectly still beside a stream, one paw raised above its head. When a school of fish glides by, it strikes, batting a victim out of the water and onto shore. At other times, the fishing cat stands belly deep in a pool, awaiting its chance. At just the right moment, it pounces. With luck, it will feel a fish pinned under its front paws. When its prize stops struggling, the fishing cat raises it to its mouth and kills it with a bite.

All cats like to be clean, and even though the fishing cat spends much time in the water, it still gives itself a good scrubbing with its rough tongue.

Does your cat wash herself?

The scientific name for the fishing cat is *Prionailurus viverrinus*. It is found throughout southern Asia and in certain islands in the South Pacific.

33

Ocelot

In the jungles of South and Central America there lives a cat whose beautiful spotted fur is the cause of all its troubles. As in the biblical story about Joseph and his brothers, this cat has been given a coat of many colors. It contains shades of rust and brown and black on a background of white or cream. Its spots are of many shapes. Some are solid dots. Others have brown centers circled by black. The coat also contains beautiful black lines. The problem is that many human beings want this coat for themselves. So, like Joseph's brothers, they plot to kill its rightful owner.

The cat we are talking about is the ocelot. It once lived in many places, for it is wonderfully adaptable. It could make its living in forests, in thorn brush, even in marshes. Now, however, it is so rare it is found only in a few dense jungles. There it sleeps by day, hunts at night, and is seldom seen. That's too bad because this cat is not only beautiful to look at, it also has many interesting traits.

For example, the ocelot is a tidy eater—so much so that it will completely pluck a bird it has killed before taking a single bite. Most cats can't wait. They pull out a few large feathers, then begin feeding, spitting out quills and plumes as they go. The ocelot also strips every bit of fur from any small animal it kills before eating it.

This lovely cat once lived in the southwestern part of the United States. Now it is gone.

Would you wear this cat's coat?

Does your cat take long naps during the daytime?

🐾 The scientific name for the ocelot is *Leopardus pardalis*. It is still found in parts of Mexico, Central America, and South America. It is a threatened species, which means that it may soon become endangered. Endangered animals are those that are on the brink of extinction.

35

Jaguarundi

The jaguarundi looks more like a marten or a mink than a cat. Its body appears to be too long for its short legs. Its head appears to be too small for its long body. Its chirping voice sounds like a bird. Anyone who mistakes this animal for something other than a cat can be excused!

The jaguarundi differs from its relatives in behavior as well as in appearance. Most adult wild cats are loners. They get together only for brief periods during mating season. Afterward each cat returns to its own hunting ground, which it then sprays with "cat repellent" to warn away intruders. This antisocial behavior ensures that each cat will find enough food to survive. Jaguarundi pairs, however, do not always split up after mating. Some remain together for long periods of time and make use of a common hunting ground.

The jaguarundi lives mainly in South and Central America, but it can also be found in Mexico and the southwestern part of the United States. In Texas and Arizona it ducks about in thorny thickets too dense for longer-legged animals to enter. In Latin America it prefers to live near marshes and streams where many birds nest. Though it is primarily a bird hunter, it also catches mice and rats. The Aztec Indians knew this. They kept jaguarundis to control pests long before Columbus discovered the New World.

The jaguarundi comes in more than one color. Some are red, and some are brownish gray, and some are black. Kittens born in the same litter can be different colors.

Were your cat's brothers and sisters all the same color?

🐾 The scientific name for the jaguarundi is *Herpailurus ya-gouarundi*. This cat lives mostly in South and Central America, but some can be found in Mexico and the southern part of the United States.

Jaguar

The jaguar is the biggest and strongest New World cat. It can drag a thousand-pound horse across rough country for more than a mile! Even its jaw muscles are powerful. They can crack open the thick skull of a bull, as if it were a walnut. For this reason, the jaguar is not afraid to take on a crocodile. No other cat will do this.

Such a mighty animal is bound to be heavyset, and indeed the jaguar is a burly-looking cat. Its thick legs, barrel-shaped chest, and big head make it look very fierce. Still, the jaguar is not especially dangerous to humans. That's because it keeps to itself and lives deep in thick jungles and sloshy marshes. Even were you to penetrate these harsh places, chances are you would fail to see a jaguar. Jaguars are good hiders. In this, they are helped by the way their spotted coats match the spatter of sunlight that filters through treetops and plays on the forest floor.

Some jaguars, like some leopards, are born black. Even so, dim spots show through their dark coats. The jaguar and the leopard have other things in common, too. Both can roar and neither can purr. Lions and tigers share this trait, which scientists regard as proof that these four cats are closely related. Yet lions and leopards live in Africa and Asia, tigers live only in Asia, and jaguars live in South and Central America.

Like its Asian cousin the tiger, the jaguar is a good swimmer and often hides near a watering hole. When animals come to drink, it

chases them beyond their depth where they are easier to kill. Sometimes jaguars swim up and down rivers looking for otters and turtles to eat. One tribe of South American Indians say that this water-loving cat attracts fish by dipping its tail in the water. When one rises to the bait, the jaguar swats it out of the water.

That's no worse a fish story than many I've heard!

Does your cat like to play with water?

🐾 The scientific name for the jaguar is *Panthera onca*. Today it is found in Mexico, Central America, and South America. Once it lived in the southwestern part of the United States. The last jaguar in the United States was shot in New Mexico in 1903.

Bobcat

If any wild cat can be said to be all American, it is the bobcat. Like our national symbol, the bald eagle, it lives nowhere else but in North America. Not long ago it could be found in forty-eight states. Only Alaska and Hawaii never had bobcats. Now many states have lost this wonderful cat, and many other states say their bobcat populations are low.

Bobcats are such good hiders that few people are fortunate enough to see one. If you should be one of those lucky people, you will know this cat at once by its tufted ears and its stump of a tail. Not being a tree-dweller, the bobcat has no need of a long tail to help it balance. Its short tail, on the other hand, serves it well. The underside is bright white and easy to see. When kittens follow their mother through dense brush or high grass, they keep their eyes on her tail, which she holds erect and waggles. That way they don't get lost.

Like many wild cats, each bobcat stakes out its own living space. It does this by spraying its pathways with scent. When strange bobcats smell these markers, they know enough to keep out. By this means

each bobcat ensures that it will find enough food to eat. If you happen to walk past a bobcat's scent marker, you will know it.

Even though the bobcat's favorite food is rabbit, it hunts other small animals as well. It is a wonderful mouser. It also catches fish and birds. The bobcat plays an important role in nature. It keeps small animals from multiplying too fast for their own good.

Does your cat hunt mice?

The scientific name for the bobcat is *Lynx rufus*. Its home is in North America, mostly in the United States.

41

Canada Lynx

The Canada lynx must like cold weather. Most of these animals live in Canada and Alaska. Some, however, live in mountainous parts of states that border Canada, where snow lasts well into summer.

In winter the lynx grows a thick coat of fur. To keep its face from freezing, it also grows long side-whiskers, called muttonchops. Even its oversized paws become covered with long fur, so much so that they give the impression that their owner is wearing galoshes. Such big

furry paws serve more than one purpose: They not only keep this cat's feet warm, they act like snowshoes and prevent the lynx from sinking into deep snowdrifts.

The lynx is a sight hunter. It spies its prey a long way off, for in the far north there are not many trees to block its view. The lynx has such good eyesight that it can see a mouse 250 feet away. It can see a snowshoe hare at 1000 feet. That's farther than the length of three football fields! Even so, with only a scattering of trees to use as cover, the lynx has a hard time sneaking up on prey. Evidently, seeing well is not enough to guarantee hunting success—just as important is not being seen.

In summer the lynx gets help from nature. When the snow melts, the lynx sheds its heavy undercoat. The fur that is left is short and matches the color of the caribou moss that blankets the ground. When a lynx lies on this ground cover, it is hardly noticeable. This good camouflage helps it catch unsuspecting animals.

The snowshoe hare is the lynx's favorite food. When snowshoe hares are plentiful, lynxes eat well and survive. In years when snowshoe hares are scarce, lynxes die off. A lynx must be a skilled hunter to make a living. For this reason, kittens stay with their mother until they are nine months old and almost as big as she is. If they cannot catch enough to eat, she brings them food.

Does your cat have long-distance vision?

The scientific name for the lynx is *Lynx canadensis*. The Canada lynx is found only in North America, but it has close relatives, also called lynx, in mountainous parts of Europe, in Russia, and in a few parts of Asia Minor. They are not quite the same though, and most, but not all, scientists regard them as separate species.

43

Puma

The first Europeans to visit the New World reported that there were lions here. Columbus wrote that he saw them in Central America. Amerigo Vespucci recorded sighting them along the coast of South America. And John Smith claimed they lived in Virginia. What these early explorers and settlers were looking at, of course, was not the African lion at all, but the puma—a large cat native to North, Central, and South America.

Their mistake was understandable. Both the male and female puma look like an African lioness. They are a quite different animal, however. For one thing, male pumas do not grow manes as male lions do. And female pumas do not form prides and help care for one another's cubs as African lionesses do. Nor do female pumas hunt together and then share their catch with their mates. A more basic difference is that pumas do not roar like lions. Their voice boxes are not made to produce that sound. Lions, on the other hand, are unable to purr like pumas. Nevertheless, for many years Dutch fur traders mistook the skins they were buying from Indian trappers for those of African lions.

One reason the misunderstanding lasted so long was that the puma is seldom seen. Its keen hearing and long legs enable it to lope ahead of noisy people coming its way. Also it is a good jumper. In a single leap, it can hide itself in the cover of a tall tree.

Actually, pumas like high places. In the West they bound up steep cliffs that many mountain climbers would not attempt. From there they watch for prey. Should a deer pass beneath a puma's lookout,

the big cat will leap onto its back and dig its huge claws and teeth into the animal's neck.

The puma is known by many names. In New England it is called a catamount. In some parts of the Midwest, it is said to be a cougar. People in Florida have named it the Florida panther. Out West this cat that looks like the King of the Beasts is called a mountain lion.

Does your cat like to watch the world from a high place?

🐾 The scientific name for the puma is *Puma concolor*. It is found in North, Central, and South America. In recent years its numbers have declined. A special race of puma found only in Florida (the Florida panther) is almost gone.

45

Your cat has many wild cousins. In this book you have met nearly half of them. Here is a list of the others:

Bornean Red Cat *Profelis badia*
Clouded Leopard *Neofelis nebulosa*
Eurasian Lynx *Lynx lynx**
European Wildcat *Felis silvestris silvestris*
Flat-Headed Cat *Prionailurus planiceps*
Geoffroy's Cat *Leopardus geoffroyi*
Golden Cat *Profelis aurata*
Indian Desert Cat *Felis silvestris ornata*
Iriomote Cat *Prionailurus iriomotensis*
Jungle Cat *Felis chaus*
✓ Kodkod *Leopardus guigna*
Leopard Cat *Prionailurus bengalensis*
Margay *Leopardus wiedi*
Mountain Cat *Oreailurus jacobita*
Oncilla, Little Spotted Cat, *Leopardus tigrinus*
Pampas Cat *Lynchailurus colocolo*
Rusty-Spotted Cat *Prionailurus rubiginosus*
Sand-Dune Cat *Felis margarita*
Spanish Lynx *Lynx pardinus**
Temminck's Cat *Profelis temmincki*

*Some scientists classify these two cats, together with the Canada lynx, as a single species.

46

Index